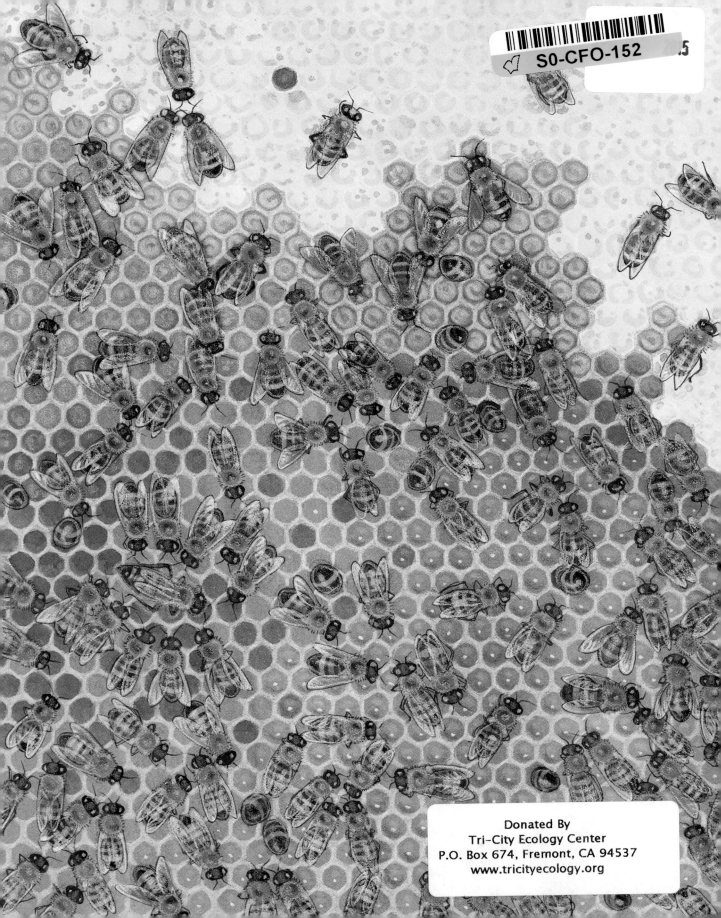

Maggie de Vries

Illustrated by Renné Benoit

Big City
Bees

GREYSTONE BOOKS

D&M PUBLISHERS INC.

Vancouver/Toronto/Berkeley

SPRING

"The trees are greening," Sophie says.
"It must be planting time."

"Not for pumpkins," says Matthew.
He looks at Grandpa. "I'm pretty sure."

"Not for pumpkins," Grandpa says.
"Pumpkins need heat. Real heat."

And bees. Pumpkins need bees.

In the big community garden, Sophie and Matthew wait for planting time. While they wait, they watch for bees—watch and worry.

"We'll need bees to make the pumpkins grow," says Matthew. "What if they don't come?"

Sophie glares at him. "They will," she says. "Of course they will." But she is worried, too.

Are there bees in the big city? Will they find the children's garden when it's time?

Far, far from the garden, honeybees live in a place that nobody knows. High in a hollow tree, deep in the city's biggest park, live thousands and thousands and thousands of bees.

Hidden in the tree, worker bees are raising
a new queen. If the old queen and the new queen
meet, they will fight to the death.

Instead, the old queen and half of her workers fly away, out of the park, straight into the big city.

Far above a busy street, they hang from a branch—a softly buzzing ball—as scouts search for just the right spot for their new home.

On that very same day, Sophie and Matthew walk downtown with Grandpa. They are searching for big city bees.

The city roars with life.

Below the bees, Sophie and Matthew look up, amazed. Above the bees, a hotel towers. The swarm has chosen its spot well. On the hotel's terrace, among beds of mint and lavender, are four hives of bees.

The beekeeper rushes from the hotel, clutching an empty box. High on a ladder, he taps the branch from which the bees hang. Dozens dart about him, angry and uncertain, but most plummet into their new home, like water falling.

The children gaze in wonder. One day, will these bees find their garden?

The beekeeper's box forms the bottom
of a new red hive.
    That box is for the queen. Each day she lays
hundreds of eggs, one in each small wax cell.
The eggs hatch into larvae, which grow and
change into new honeybees.

Two boxes stacked on top are for honey. The
bees fly through the city, searching, searching.
When they find flowers, they alight, collecting
nectar to fill the comb and pollen to feed the larvae.
As they collect the pollen, some of it falls into the
female flowers and pollinates them.

SUMMER

Hot at last. Planting time!

Sophie and Matthew's spot is in a corner near the compost heap, beside the corn plants and the beans.

"Pumpkins love compost," Grandpa tells them, "and corn. And beans." Grandpa knows everything about growing.

Sophie and Matthew mix compost into the soil. They soak the ground. Together, they mound the earth into a small hill.

Sophie shakes two pumpkin seeds into her brother's palm and two into her own. They push each seed into the earth, add some water, and watch the sun beat down.

On their way home, they see three bees buzzing around a blackberry bush.

"They're gathering honey," Matthew says.

"Not honey—nectar," Sophie replies. "They're gathering pollen, too. Look at that one! She's got pollen everywhere!"

Back at the hive, the store of honey grows.

Forager bees return with bellies filled with nectar and, on their hind legs, baskets packed with pollen. Inside their bodies, they turn the nectar into honey. They fill the cells with pollen to feed the growing larvae.

Summer is passing.

Will the bees come when the pumpkin flowers bloom?

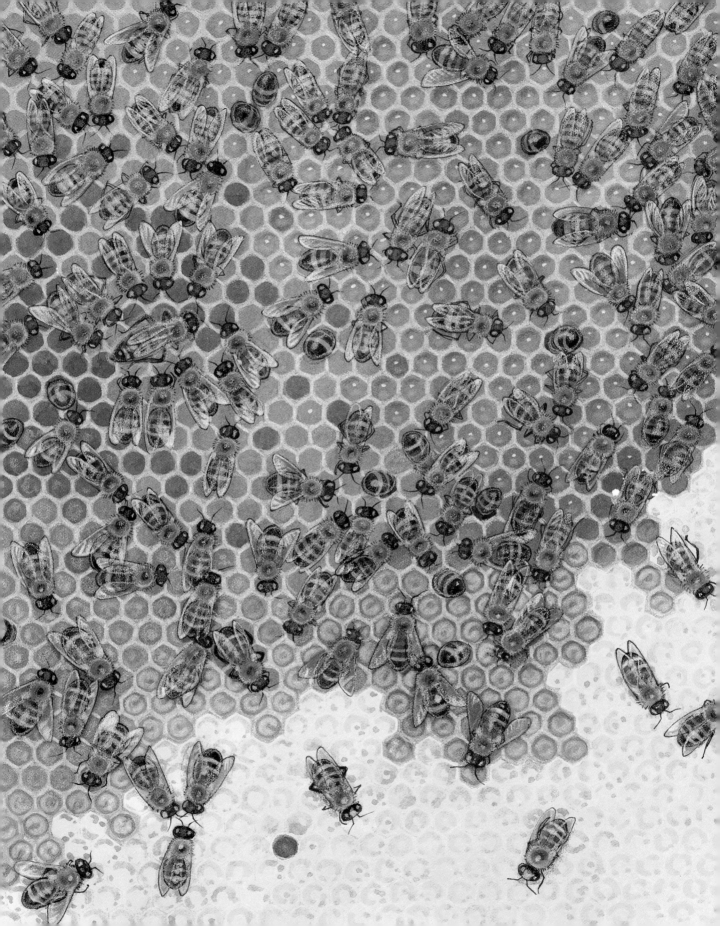

"Look!" Sophie says to Matthew.

He looks, and there they are, tiny green shoots, two small leaves on each. The pumpkin plants are growing.

"They look like butterflies," Matthew says.

Two weeks later, the vines have spread. The leaves are big and round.

Every day, Sophie and Matthew visit the garden and tend to their plants.

And every day, they look for bees.

Sophie pulls aside a leaf. "Matthew," she shouts, "a flower!"

The buds are everywhere—tiny and new, golden yellow on long, thin stems.

Grandpa looks. "Those are the males," he says. "The females will come out soon." He places the leaf back on top. "They only bloom for one day," he adds, "beginning at dawn."

Two days later, against the vine, more golden buds appear, resting on the bulbous hint of green pumpkins. The females are about to bloom.

Without bees to pollinate them, the pumpkins will not grow.

Will the bees come? Will they?

Sophie and Matthew rise before the sun. They bundle up against the early-morning chill and grab a pair of binoculars and a flashlight. Grandpa follows.

The park is dark and still. Matthew lifts a massive leaf and shines the light on the pumpkin flowers. They are furled tight. Beeless.

The children settle down to wait. Sophie holds her knees close. "Come on, bees," she whispers.

Minutes pass. Half an hour. The sky grows light. Slowly, slowly, the petals unfurl.

"Please come, bees," says Matthew. "Please!"

At last, in the same moment, they see it. One bee.

A honeybee buzzes over the closest flower. Breaths held, the children watch.

And, as if by magic, four more bees arrive. The flowers are huge, like goblets. The bees are frenzied, sipping nectar, gathering pollen. In and out they crawl—first into the male flowers, then the females. Inside the female flowers, pollen brushes off the bees' bodies, fertilizing the plants so the pumpkins can begin to form.

Not much time is left. The female flowers will close up by noon.

Sophie and Matthew watch as two of the honeybees fly away.

The bees fly back along the railway tracks, up to the mint and lavender terrace, and into the big red hive. Bodies fat with pollen, bellies filled with nectar, they dance to tell the other bees exactly where the flowers are.

Fourteen bees fly off toward the garden.
They must be quick. Already some of the flowers
are folding up their petals.

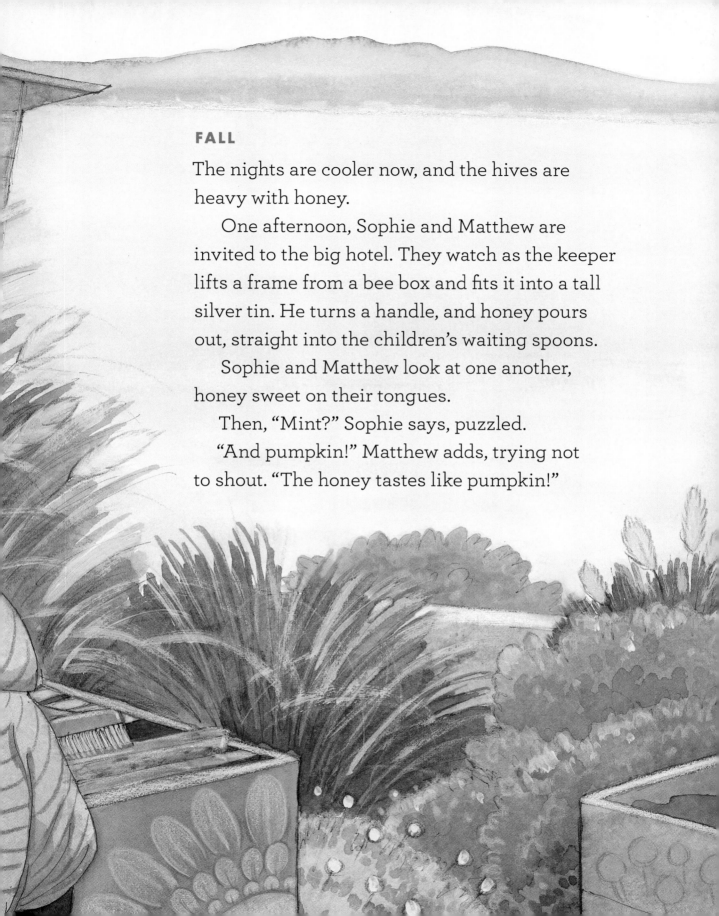

FALL

The nights are cooler now, and the hives are heavy with honey.

One afternoon, Sophie and Matthew are invited to the big hotel. They watch as the keeper lifts a frame from a bee box and fits it into a tall silver tin. He turns a handle, and honey pours out, straight into the children's waiting spoons.

Sophie and Matthew look at one another, honey sweet on their tongues.

Then, "Mint?" Sophie says, puzzled.

"And pumpkin!" Matthew adds, trying not to shout. "The honey tastes like pumpkin!"

At Halloween, eleven pumpkins are heavy on
the vines.

Sophie and Matthew pick the biggest, roundest
pair for themselves.

WINTER

Frosty mornings. The jack-o'-lanterns collapse
on the front step. In the garden, the children turn
the dead plants into the earth, spread black soil
over them, and dump the old pumpkins into the
compost.

On the terrace, the big red hive is quiet. The bees have done their foraging.

Next year, when the pumpkin plants bloom, will the bees come again? Will they pollinate the flowers so the children's pumpkins can grow?

Will they?

WHY DO BEES MATTER?

> Bees make the honey that we all love. But they do much, much more.

> Just like Sophie and Matthew, we need bees to make our plants grow. Bees pollinate one-third of our food plants—such as strawberries, apples, tomatoes, peaches, and almonds.

> Bees are disappearing. Lately, many beekeepers have found their hives empty. Around the world, people are working hard to discover why the bees are dying and what we can do to save them.

HOW CAN YOU AND YOUR FAMILY HELP BEES?

> Plant native, bee-friendly plants that flower at different times of the year, so that bees can always find food. Find out from a local beekeepers group which plants in your area bees love the most.

> Replace part of your lawn with flowering plants. Lawns are like deserts to bees.

> Bees need water every day, but they can drown in pools and ponds with steep sides. Create a water garden with plants bees can stand on while they drink. You can find out more about water gardens for bees in books or on the Internet.

BUZZ, BUZZ, BUZZ

> The buzzing of bees is the sound of their wings flapping—about 200 times per second!

> A hive of honeybees will fly as far as 300,000 kilometers (200,000 miles) to collect enough nectar to make just half a kilogram (one pound) of honey. A hive can contain 50,000 bees.

> Honeybees are one of more than 20,000 kinds of bees. How many different kinds can you spot on the flowers in your neighborhood?

> People have been collecting honey since prehistoric times. And we've been keeping bees in hives for well over 2,000 years. Before we learned to take sugar from sugarcane, we depended on honey to make things sweet. Back then, honey was very, very valuable!

*To Dianne Wells and Reg Kienast, the first
to share with me the wonders of bees*—MdV

For my grandma—RB

· ·

Greystone Books
An imprint of D&M Publishers Inc.
2323 Quebec Street, Suite 201
Vancouver BC Canada V5T 4S7
www.greystonebooks.com

Cataloguing data available from Library and Archives Canada
ISBN 978-1-55365-906-8 (cloth)
ISBN 978-1-77100-051-2 (pbk.)
ISBN 978-1-55365-907-5 (ebook)

Editing by Kathy Vanderlinden
Jacket and interior design by Jessica Sullivan
Jacket illustrations by Renné Benoit
Printed and bound in China by C&C Offset Printing Co., Ltd.
Text printed on acid-free paper
Distributed in the U.S. by Publishers Group West

We gratefully acknowledge the financial support of the Canada Council
for the Arts, the British Columbia Arts Council, the Province of British
Columbia through the Book Publishing Tax Credit, and the Government
of Canada through the Canada Book Fund for our publishing activities.

ACKNOWLEDGMENTS

I would like to thank Graeme Evans, who showed me bees in the big city, and everyone at Vancouver's Fairmont Waterfront Hotel, who welcomed me when I wanted to learn more about bees. I would also like to thank everyone at Greystone Books for believing in this project, and for the brilliant work they do.

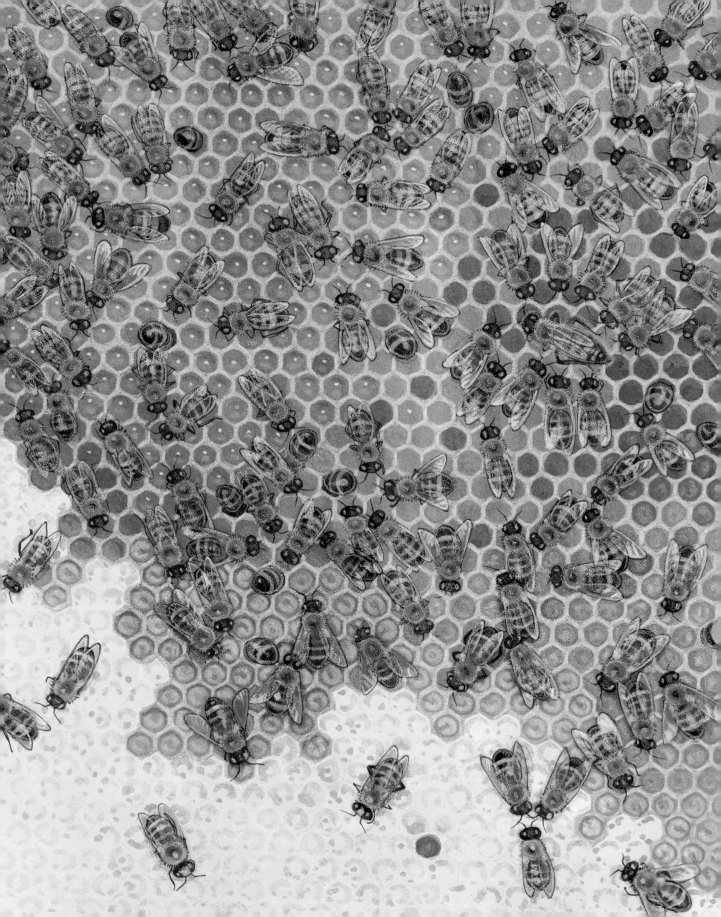